The Seamstress

by

José María de Pereda

Rise of Douai

Copyright © 2014 Rise of Douai

All rights reserved.

ISBN-13:
978-1505753707

ISBN-10:
1505753708

Introduction

José María de Pereda (February 6, 1833, Polanco, Cantabria — March 1, 1906, Polanco) was one of the most distinguished of modern Spanish novelists, and a Member of the Royal Spanish Academy.

He was educated at the Institute Cántabro of Santander, whence he went in 1852 to Madrid, where he studied with the vague purpose of entering the artillery corps. Abandoning this design after three years' trial, he returned home and began his literary career by contributing articles to a local journal, La Abeja montañesa in 1858. He also wrote much in a weekly paper, El Tío Cayetín, and in 1864 he collected his powerful realistic sketches of local life and manners under the title of Escenas montañesas ("Mountain scenes").

Pereda fought against the revolution of 1868 in El Tío Cayetín, writing the newspaper almost single-handed. In 1871 he was elected as the Carlist deputy for Cabuérniga. In this same year he published a second series of Escenas montañesas under the title of Tipos y paisajes; and in 1876 appeared Bocetos al temple, three tales, in one of which the author describes his disenchanting political experiences.

The Tipos trashumantes belongs to the year 1877, as does El Buey suelto, which was intended as a reply to the thesis of Balzac's work, Les Petites misères de la vie conjugale. More and more pessimistic as to the political future of his country, Pereda took occasion in Don Gonzalo González de la Gonzalera (1879) to ridicule the Revolution as he had seen it at work, and to pour scorn upon the nouveaux riches who exploited Liberalism for their personal ends. Two novels by his friend Pérez Galdós, Doña Perfecta and Gloria, drew from Pereda a reply, De Tal palo tal astilla (1880), in which he endeavours to show that tolerance in religious matters is disastrous alike to nations and to individuals. The Esbozos y rasguños (1881) is of lighter material, and is less attractive than El Sabor de la Tierruca (1882), a striking piece of landscape which won immediate appreciation.

New ground was broken in Pedro Sánchez (1883), where Pereda leaves his native province to portray the disillusion of a sincere enthusiast who has plunged into the political life of the capital. Pereda's masterpiece is Sotileza (1884), a vigorous rendering of marine life by an artist who perceives and admires the daily heroisms of his fisher-folk. It has often been alleged against the author that he confines himself to provincial life, to lowly personages and to unrefined subjects, and no doubt an anxiety to clear himself from this absurd reproach led him to attempt a description of society at the capital in La Montálvez (1888), which is certainly the least interesting of his performances. In La Puchera (1889) he returned to the marine subjects which he knew and loved best. Again, in Peñas arriba (1895), the love of country life is manifested in the masterly contrast between the healthy, moral labor of the fields and the corrupt, squalid life of cities.

Pereda's fame was now established; the statutes of the Spanish Academy, which require members to reside at Madrid, were suspended in his favor (1896). But his literary career was over. The death of his eldest son, the disastrous campaign in Cuba and the Philippines (during the Spanish-American

War), darkened his closing years, and his health failed long before his death.

The Seamstress

"How pretty you are to-day, Theresa."

"Oh, nonsense!"

"But it's true, though! that kerchief of pink crepe against your white throat."

"Oh, you're joking!"

"And your hair is as black as your eyes, did you know it?"

"You flatterer!"

"And such a slender little figure, in such a gracefully draped gown! That's an awfully pretty muslin, you know!"

"You don't say so!"

"You see I am very fond of lilac. It always was a favorite color of mine. And then it falls so prettily over a dainty shoe, when it's as tiny as yours is. My, what a cunning foot it is, to be sure! If you would put it just a trifle further out... so!"

"Well, well, listen to this!"

"I would like to have your photograph, in just that position, but looking up at me,... so!"

"What taste you have!"

"To be sure I have! And why not?"

"I'd have you know I've been photographed already."

"Indeed?"

"And by Pica-Groom."

"In the position I like?"

"Mercy on us, no! I'm in my ball-dress I had on Sunday when you met us near the gas factory."

"And nothing would induce you to look at me, Theresa! You were having such fun!"

"There were eight or nine of us!"

"Oh, surely nine, Theresa. You seemed to me the nine Muses, all in one graceful band together!"

"Oh, get along with you! You are always laughing at people and calling them names!"

"But among those trees, and going up that hill... Mount Helicon, of course..."

"Where is that?"

"Mount Helicon? Oh, it's a little beyond Torrelavega. But what I did not like about it was that Apollo who went with you."

"His name was not Pollo. He's a clerk..."

"I thought as much... I mean he seemed somewhat commonplace, while you were all so airy, fairy, beautiful!"

"There, now you're at it again! Yes, we were going to the ball at Miranda, as we do every Sunday."

"Yes, I heard the organ."

"And the man who was with us was one of the set who gets up the balls. And as he had given me tickets for all the summer dances in the garden, and if it comes handy will invite us for the winter ones, too, in the hall..."

"Yes, I know these impresarios and their friends are very gallant fellows. They pay, that you may dance all the year round, for nothing."

"Just so! And we are just as good as the ladies who do the same thing!"

"Of course you are!"

"It seems to me that the 'Cream and Flower' and the 'Organ' have no reason to envy any other dancing-place."

"Above all, in pretty faces and lively dancers!"

"As you say, it is..."

"What I said, or was just going to say is, that because you were going to a dance was no reason for not bowing on the street."

"Goodness! What would people say?"

"How do you mean that, 'What would people say'?"

"Why, that's clear enough! What would people say to your knowing us?"

"You say that with a tone..."

"No, no, not at all; but it's true, for all that."

"Nonsense! I bow to everybody on the street, and enjoy it, and above all when I meet you!"

"Thank you, but..."

"But what?"

"Well, I don't believe you, there! You're a great joker... and well, to tell the plain truth, I don't feel any confidence in you."

"Ah, there we have it! But why should you not trust me? Surely, you don't take me for a gay deceiver, do you?"

"Oh no, but the men in your set and you yourself are great gossips."

"You are hard on me, Theresa!"

"I'm sorry for it, I'm sure, but I always tell the truth. When you passed us on Sunday one of the girls and I were talking of that very thing."

"The one who was walking on your right?"

"What made you guess her?"

"Because she pleased me so much, the witty red-head!"

"So you're taken with the Anvil?"

"And why Anvil, if I may ask!"

"Stupid! That's what they call the girl."

"And why do they call her so?"

"Because her father is a blacksmith."

"Heavens! What a name!"

"And the one who was walking on my left, don't you know her name either?"

"No, my dear."

"Well, where do you keep yourself, anyway?"

"At least this will prove how unjust you were before, when you doubted my sincerity!"

"For all that I thought every one knew Beanie."

"I do not know her by that name. And how did she come by it?"

"Why, her mother sells beans in the Square."

"How atrocious!"

"Oh, we all have nicknames of that sort. And now you're beginning to see daylight, eh?"

"I assure you I am. And who has amused himself with baptizing you all in this fashion?"

"Well, when we were being taught as little girls, and then later at the dances, there's always some one who, for the sake of joking with us a bit, gives us a nickname, and as ill weeds grow apace..."

"What a notion! And among yourselves you go by these names?"

"Not a bit of it! Still, we know them, and as they are no disgrace..."

"Of course... but to return to our red-head."

"You seem to think of no one else."

"As you said you were talking about me..."

"I said that?"

"At least, you said something very like it."

"What I said was that we were talking about the way some men had of boasting about things that had never happened to them."

"I'm sure that doesn't hit me."

"No, certainly not, but some of the men you know very well."

"It may be so. And do you know, Theresa, that for some time the red-head has been putting on all sorts of airs and graces."

"Didn't I tell you!"

"Oh, I say it with no thought of injuring the girl."

"That's the way all these things are said, and then the Evil One is in it! If a girl is a little dressed up some fine day, my, how they talk! It's plain enough that you are used to hearing that a lady must spend a small fortune to present a decent appearance on the street, and as we have no income, the moment you see us spruced up a bit you think at once we have presents given us... as they should not be given. Neither the redhead nor I have anything but the twenty cents we earn by sewing at the houses where we are employed, and the cup of chocolate they give us for breakfast and supper, as you know. But we know our trade, and with two yards of tulle and six yards of dimity we make a dress that those who do not understand such things think must be worth a lot of money. Take the one I have on now... it will wear for four summers, and who knows how much longer, if water and soap and irons are still left us! So there you have it!"

"I think so, too, my dear."

"Of course, this girl is naturally showy, and has some style, and then she has a wonderful knack at cutting and sewing. She can make a ball-dress just out of old skirts..."

"I never said anything to the contrary, you know."

"And seeing her dressed for the street, as she has good looks and a pretty figure... uf! the least they think is that it was bought with bad money. And that you may know how things really are, the poor girl has to provide her father's smoking tobacco out of that same twenty cents! But of course, it's only a poor little seamstress... and so it goes on! And if I were to tell all I know... how many silk dresses rustle through these streets that have never been paid for, and how many, too, that have been paid for, without the husbands of the ladies that wear them being a bit the poorer! But they are fine ladies, and are pardoned in advance for all their sins... and so it is with other things... how many of the graceful figures you admire so much have been made with these two hands! But I guess I'd better stop right there."

"You are unkind, Theresa! What I said about the red-head was just for the sake of saying something. For the last three or four days, when she went by at noontime in the Old Square, I noticed she was more dressed than usual, and..."

"That means you go there on purpose to watch her go by."

"I won't say that I go to see her, but perhaps to see her, you, and the others, yes."

"And what do you get out of it, anyway?"

"It does my eyes good! It really does! You are so pretty, one and all of you! But I must say I am deeply shocked to notice how you all manage to pass through the Square, no matter where you come from or where you are going to."

"Well, I suppose all roads lead to Rome, don't

they?... and when we leave off sewing for an hour at noon, we take half of it to see people, and get a little fresh air."

"And what a pretty friend of yours that was that stopped you this morning at the corner of the street! But she is not so stylish as you are."

"Oh, you mean a very dark girl? She's not a friend of mine... she sews for a tailor."

"Oh, I see; but as you were talking with her..."

"She was just giving me a message. And it isn't that I don't care to be friendly with some of them, but you see that we who go out to do fine sewing keep ourselves to ourselves. And don't go and think we haven't good reason to set ourselves up above them... look at the way the dressmakers treat us! My, you'd think they were doing us an honor when they bow to us on the street."

"What a wise sly-boots it is, to be sure!"

"And now I think of it, what were you saying this morning to that gentleman with whiskers, when we went by, and you were staring so?"

"So you saw me?"

"Oh, I see all I want to, and more too!"

"You are a pretty little mischief-maker, Theresa! I shall take that as a warning. Well, then, I was saying to my friend that you were all so much prettier when you went out with nothing on your head, with your hair so beautifully done up, and those fetching little kerchiefs round your necks, like the one you have on now, than when you wear a mantilla and shawl, which hide the graceful outlines."

"My eye, what a lot you see!"

"Of course we do!"

"But they don't all of them wear a mantilla."

"And you are one of the exceptions, and I warn you now, so that you may never make the mistake of putting one on."

"And where's the harm, anyway?"

"With the mantilla you would cease to be an exceedingly pretty type of the pure Santander race, and would simply be lost in the common crowd of young ladies all more or less far from chic."

"Some of my friends can wear a veil as well as anybody."

"But you see a veil is never becoming, because while it does not really cover an ugly face, it hides a pretty one, and then it requires a shawl, which conceals the figure."

"My goodness! What a lot you know about it all!"

"I am an artist, Theresa."

"And what are you driving at, after all?"

"Mere trifles. I study beauty wherever I find it."

"It seems to me that what you are studying is just pure mischief!"

"That is not true! Nor is it an argument in favor of wearing veils."

"Well, I don't like them, either, but they're the fashion. But what are you staring at so, through the window?"

"What makes you blush like that?"

"I, blush? Goodness! Perhaps you think it's because of that young fellow in the doorway over there!"

"You are defending yourself before you are accused, Theresa."

"You see, you might be fancying it was something else, and as the lad is more or less on my mind... and he's a real good fellow too."

"You are not telling me the truth, Theresa. I know him very well, and I know he would not be waiting every day at this hour, if he did not hope..."

"Has the good-for-nothing been telling you what is not true?"

"On my word of honor, we have not mentioned the subject."

"You see, that sort of thing happens so often. And now let me tell you, so you needn't go thinking something that is not true, that I do like the lad. But he is just losing his time."

"I do not understand."

"Well, a year ago he danced with me at the 'Cream and Flower.' And ever since then, I don't know how, he finds out where I am going to sew. But I am sure to meet him this way every evening when I leave off work, above all in winter, when we go out at nightfall... and that is what worries me."

"That he goes with you after dark?"

"No; that he seems to care less about going with me in the daytime."

"Then what is he about, over opposite?"

"Oh, he's waiting for me. But when we get to the

corner of the street, he will make some excuse, and off he goes! And when I am at work on the Mole, or any central street, he waits for me in the same doorway, then we talk for a while, and then... each one goes off on his own hook. You see there is no real pleasure in this sort of thing, and for that reason I like my own kind better."

"And who are they?"

"Oh, the office clerks. We understand each other perfectly, and if some day,... well, you know what I mean,... it's all between poor folks. But with these fine fellows, it's a more serious affair, and woe be unto the unhappy girl who is tempted by one of them! What she has to go through with, first with him and then with the family, as if she it were who had been running after him! You know how it all comes about; it all begins in fun, and as it generally happens that the girl is foolish and believes what they tell her, she finds out too late to turn back... and that's why I tell you that young man is wasting his time."

"I believe just the contrary, as you yourself say that sometimes the girl has faith, in spite of everything."

"Well, you see I have profited by another's experience. For I have a friend... oh, the unhappy girl! When I think of the tears she has shed, and the way her father abused her!... and then the esteem she has lost through one of those rascals who deceived her! No, no, poor I was born and poor I'll remain. I don't care, for one, to be made a lady at that price!"

"And quite right you are about it. But with all this you don't dismiss your adorer, I notice."

"Oh, there's no danger so far, and there never will be;... not if I know myself, and I think I do."

"Yes, I think you do!"

"You see, we've agreed not to take any notice of these swells,... but the time for the dances comes round, and as you know, they all go to the dances. For that's a queer thing about our balls... all the men who go to the ladies' balls come to ours too, and a good many more beside. Then you see they dance with us, say such pretty things, and then... what can a girl do? Of course..."

"And all this amounts to saying that the young man yonder will not quite waste his time."

"It seems to me you are in the same boat!"

"Oh, Theresa! Would that I could be! Though it would be hard to go shares..."

"Why so?"

"Because you are so very pretty!"

"Ah, now you're going to flirt with me?"

"Yes, if you will play back!"

"And what if I tell the red-head?"

"I don't care to know her, except by sight."

"Anyway, I don't care for you."

"Thank you for your fine frankness!"

"You have a bad opinion of women."

"If they all treated me as you do, I should have a fair excuse!"

"Now you've made me break a needle."

"Never mind, I'll give you a whole package."

"At this rate I shan't get this shirt done in a week."

"So much the better. I shall see you all the oftener."

"And the work will cost you a pretty penny."

"At this price you may keep on making me shirts forever!"

"If you don't haggle about the time, then, I'm going to rob you to-day of a quarter of an hour."

"To chat with me? even if you took half a day..."

"No, no, just to go to a shop near High Street, to buy... a penny's worth of dried fruits,[1] which I adore."

"Come, come, none of your tricks, Theresa!"

"As she gets them from Castille by wholesale, the shop woman, a friend of mine, gives me many more for a penny than they do in other shops. Don't you like them yourself?"

"No!"

"My! how queer! Will you please hand me that bit of tape down there near you, to tie up my work with?... Thank you... but how bad your face does look, all of a sudden!"

"Well, you see I have... a swelling on my gum..."

"And didn't it hurt you before?"

"Not so much as it does now, no."

"Then you'd better try a dried fig... they're awfully good for swellings."

"Thanks, so much!"

"And now good-bye. I'm off to buy my dried fruit."

"Good-bye, and good luck to you!"

To write a volume about the habits and customs of these mountain people without dedicating some pages to the seamstress, would be depriving Santander of one of its chief features. So important and conspicuous is this part of the population that the weaker sex there, after making some necessary exceptions, might be divided in equal parts between women who are seamstresses and those who are not. But to write of the habits of the former would be a great exposure for a person like myself who does not know them well. To be mistaken in the slightest detail would cost him dear! In short, gentle reader, I have a certain healthy respect for this seamstress class, and would hardly like to run the risk of painting her portrait.

And granting that "the style is the man," and therefore the woman too, study well this dialogue, which is true to life. See what you can make out of it, and govern yourself accordingly afterward, if Theresa considers herself injured by your deductions; in this case I assure you she would be guilty of injustice. For my own part, I am protected from her wrath by being able to say,—if I am hard put to it,—"You yourself have said it." Tu es auctor.

Notes:

1. To understand to the full the subtle repartee that follows, it should be explained at this point that the word orejones may mean either a box of dried fruits or a box on the ear.

THE END

RISE OF DOUAI

RISE OF DOUAI

TWITTER : @RISEOFDOUAI

© 2013, PUBLISHED BY RISE OF DOUAI PUBLISHING, OTHER PUBLICATIONS:

- AN IDIOT'S GUIDE TO: BEE HUNTING BY JOHN LOCKARD, EDITED BY ARSALAN AHMED (2012)(PAPERBACK) ISBN-10: 1478383550

- THE RISE OF DOUAI BY ARSALAN AHMED (2012)(PAPERBACK) ISBN-10: 1479267783

- THE RICHEST MAN IN BABYLON BY GEORGE S. CLASON (2012) (PAPERBACK) ISBN-10: 1479377341

- THINK AND GROW RICH BY NAPOLEON HILL (2012) (PAPERBACK) ISBN-10: 1480061638

- AS A MAN THINKETH BY MR JAMES ALLEN (2012) (PAPERBACK) ISBN-10: 1480088161
- HOW TO ANALYZE PEOPLE ON

SIGHT BY ELSIE BENEDICT (PAPERBACK) ISBN-10: 1480081272
- THE ART OF WAR BY MR SUN TZU (PAPERBACK) ISBN-10: 1480082007
- MACBETH BY MR WILLIAM SHAKESPEARE (PAPERBACK) ISBN-10: 1480060682
- A CHRISTMAS CAROL BY MR CHARLES DICKENS ISBN-10: 1481194755
- CREATING CAPITAL: MONEY-MAKING AS AN AIM IN BUSINESS BY MR FREDRICK L LIPMAN ISBN-10: 1481158996
- GETTING GOLD: A PRACTICAL TREATISE FOR PROSPECTORS, MINERS, AND STUDENTS BY MR JOSEPH COLIN FRANCIS JOHNSON ISBN-10: 1481090984
- THE INTERPRETATION OF DREAMS BY MR SIGMUND FREUD ISBN-10: 1481134558
- THE COMMUNIST MANIFESTO BY MR KARL MARX AND MR FRIDRICK ENGLES ISBN-10:

1480112445
- THE PRINCE BY MR NICCOLO MACHIAVELLI ISBN-10: 1480119601
- THE WAY TO WEALTH BY MR BENJAMIN FRANKLIN ISBN-10: 1480099651

- THE ART OF MONEY GETTING - OR GOLDEN RULES FOR MAKING MONEY (SUCCESS PRINCIPLES) BY MR PHINEAS TAYLOR BARNUM ISBN-10: 1480138622

Twitter : **@RiseofDouai**

Twitter : **@RiseofDouai**